MAGIC AND MYTH

MAGIC AND MYTH

SHORT STORIES

KATHRYN TRATTNER

Ebook ISBN: 979-8-9872112-0-5

Paperback ISBN: 979-8-9872112-1-2

www.kathryntrattner.com

Editor: Jeanine Harrell - Indie Edits with Jeanine

Cover Designer: JV Arts

The ache for home lives in all of us.

— MAYA ANGELOU

CONTENTS

TORNADO

I invited the Tornado inside because, really, where else could he go? He growled, like a train vibrating in the distance, and I shivered, remembering summer nights with bugs so thick they fogged the stars, a shrill whistle calling out.

Maybe he just needed a good dinner, a second helping, and he sat, joining Winter at my table. Winter drank coffee, black and bitter, two days old and reheated in the microwave. This was the last cup, he said, before the long drive north. Spring lurked, seen in the neon green buds, but had not yet come in, not stopped by, not while everything throbbed with heat and that *newness* seeped up from red dirt.

I made pasta, only good at boiling water and heating up the contents of a jar, with no patience for anything else. We ate, and in my mouth, the taste of tomatoes and burned coffee lingered.

The Tornado complained, desirous of something solid to suck up; brick and stone, two-by-fours and good vinyl siding. But I shoveled a third and fourth helping on his plate. By sunset, he'd eaten a second pot, and I rolled him through my front door, slow and satisfied, into a night containing a sharp chartreuse that I wanted to bring to bed and fall asleep beside.

Inside, Winter promised to leave after one more cup of coffee.

BLACKBERRY BABY

Summer had a way of holding on in the South Carolina backwoods. Clinging to the edges of the low country and remaining strong. It came—saltwater on the air when the wind blew in from the coast, scents of pine and kudzu as it sighed through inland woods from the West. Languid or blustery, Summer always carried birdsong and distant voices. But when it swirled to a stop—the air died down and gave up, and the sun hovered high in a clear sky over my house—it smelled like blackberries.

———

I watched the woman pick her way down the dirt track to my house one early evening—golden skies hinting at violet, a thin sliver of moon suspended like a cutout, a window to a bright, calm place. The drink in my hand sweated, ice melting slowly, watering down the bourbon and mint. I rocked back in the chair, letting it carry me forward, knees creaking with the rattan.

She had brown hair and pale eyes, a shade borrowed from the throats of morning glories—a true pale, clear blue rarely seen. When she spoke, hesitant and wary, she clasped her hands together to keep them from taking flight, to keep her thoughts ordered. I could see it all on her, feel it even ten feet away.

"Are you Gwen Simmons?" she asked.

"I am." I swallowed the last drink, the bite diluted, flecks of muddled mint sticking to the glass. "And you are?"

"I'm Emily Madison. I was hoping to talk to you about something."

"You want to come in and tell me what's on your mind?"

I stood, gesturing to the front door, holding it as she stepped inside.

With a nod, she looked around as if she'd expected it to be darker, gloomier. I smiled, glancing at the white walls covered in photos—gaggles of distant family, past and present, every relative you could imagine. The carpet was a patterned tangle of green vines and roses, worn down in the middle, well-loved and irreplaceable. Little tables stood here and there, knickknacks on display, porcelain figures and bud vases holding sunflowers from the backyard.

The house curled in on her, walls and floors, the crystal chandelier over our heads tinkling. It was as curious as I was about the question she carried here with her heavy, a weight pulling us all toward an unknown vortex. In the kitchen, I had a clearer picture. Her desperation tasted like gasoline and lit matches, a hint of burning plastic thrown in.

"You want a glass of water?" I asked, heading for the cabinet and grabbing two glasses before she could respond.

"Sure, thank you."

"Ice?"

"Yeah, please. That would be great."

I nodded, moving slowly, the room gently spinning around this woman and her unspoken request. It was coming. She was fighting to hold it in, to keep from blurting it out and being rude. She didn't want to offend me; I could tell that by looking at her. She had a hopeful expression over pain.

Ice tumbled into the glasses piece by piece, the refrigerator groaning—appliances, house, and myself all aging gracefully together. She watched me openly, staring, searching my face for the person she'd been expecting to find.

Maybe she'd expected a young woman covered in tattoos with black nail polish or a middle-aged flower child with a flowing skirt and hemp sandals. Instead, she'd found a woman in her early sixties with salt-and-pepper hair and gold-rimmed glasses hiding dark eyes. Neither fat nor thin, comfortable in skin worn in and wrinkled, maybe a little too much sun, a mole on the corner of her mouth; a beauty mark on an aging beauty, signs of a life well-lived, the hint of something other in the way the woman moved, the way the air crackled around her.

But it was just me.

I didn't mind surprising her; it was funny, after all these years, to still be confronting whatever people's expectations might be. There had been one or two visitors who'd been convinced I might cackle and ride a broom at midnight. Maybe I needed to figure out how to make that happen. I smiled, setting the water in front of her, glass clicking against the scrubbed table, condensation already gathering.

"So, tell me," I said, easing into the chair across from

her and sipping water, rinsing the taste of gasoline from my tongue. "How do you think I can help?"

"I don't know if you can," she spoke softly, reaching out to touch the glass without picking it up. "But my friend said I needed to talk to you."

"Friend?"

"Oh," Emily looked up, smiling for the first time. "Anna. Her name is Anna. She's come to see you before."

I sucked in a breath, caught off guard by the beauty of her smile, the way it changed her face, lifting the gauntness of her cheeks. Not only a physical smile but a mental one, spiritual. A smile to light up any room. My kitchen felt brighter with her in it.

"Anna is lovely, isn't she?"

Anna had come to me to bring some peace into her life, lay old hurts to rest, and open the way for love and happiness. But that was a years ago, before Danny had died, before the world shifted around me.

"She said you were able to help her and it changed everything."

I listened to Emily's tone and the emotion behind the words more than the words themselves. There was genuine kindness in this woman, the way she spoke of her friend, the happiness at her finding peace. No secret jealousies or harbored grudges, nothing dark clinging to her, trailing her movements through the air like fine-spun spider silk.

"But why are you here?"

Keeping my voice gentle, I glanced out at the curious dusk watching us through the kitchen window; violet sunset faded, hints of deep gray around the treetops, the warm light from the house holding it all off. When she didn't respond right away, I set my glass down and leaned toward her, elbows on the table, as close as I could get. I watched the muscles in her face shift, eyes turn down. She reached for the water glass and took a sip, hand shaking the whole time.

"I want a baby."

Sitting back, surprised by such a large request, I shook my head.

"Before you say anything," she said, holding up a hand. "Let me tell you the whole thing. Please."

"Okay."

I held my breath against the smell of desperation now, the sorrow, all of it so overpowering I wanted to move the conversation outside. But she seemed fragile, needing the protection of the kitchen table, the security of the water glass. If I moved her, she might not share her story, and I wanted to know how that want had brought Emily through the woods to my house.

"I've seen every doctor. I've tried every treatment. Whatever the doctors offered, whatever a natural healer offered. I've changed everything about my life, all of it, and nothing. It's not happened for me."

"What about your husband?"

Tension coiled through the space between us, a snake rattling its tail and poised to strike. I knew from the way she held herself what the answer was, and I was sorry I'd asked.

"Gone. He was tested too. He wasn't the problem."

"Were the doctors able to tell you why you couldn't conceive?"

"No. In every way they can measure, I'm healthy."

My insides twisted for her, an ache settling like stones in my heart.

"Can you help me?"

"I can't change anything about your body, the way you're made."

She was nodding, already expecting the *no*. It was on the tip of my tongue, there at the back of my throat. A single tear ran down her cheek, and she swiped it away. I swallowed the negative response, swallowed it whole without a second thought, and reached across the table, hand outstretched, palm up.

"I'm sorry," she whispered, taking my hand. "I told myself I wasn't going to cry."

"You don't have to be sorry."

Her hand in mine was warm and soft. It had been such a long time since I'd touched another living person. And then it had been mourners offering me condolences and love, caring expressed through contact, arms and hands and shared tears. I offered that to Emily, all those things that had been fed into me I returned, passed on, to someone else in need.

She nodded. "Thanks. I didn't really expect you could, but Anna said I should ask."

"I can help you."

"What?"

Incredulity lit up her face, crazy hope and surprise mixing and flowing into her expression. The room changed, the taste going sweet like cherry pop rocks and apple blossoms, bubbled like sparkling water, fizzing between us.

"But there has to be an exchange, one thing for another."

"I understand."

I wondered if she really did. If I did. I would have to give something too; something of mine would have to be in this spell to see it into being. The offering would have to come from both of us. We would be forever bound together. I pushed back in my chair with a squeak, nodding and already thinking about what I might need.

"Come back in a week," I said. "Bring three things that speak to you, that bring to mind the things you want to welcome into your life." I tapped my lip, considering what else it might take—ritual, spell, or potion. There were other things, physical things, I would need, but not yet. Those could wait.

"I will," she said, rising with me, eyes shining.

"Good." I walked her to the door and touched her shoulder briefly on the front porch as she went down the steps—a blessing as I sent her out into the lengthening evening, down the dirt track to where her car waited. "I'll see you in a week."

———

The pressure in the house changed. I tasted curiosity, sour citrus, and clover honey. I knew the question before it left his mouth, though I didn't have an answer. Not even for myself. I couldn't bring myself to put those words out into the world.

"What made you change your mind?" Danny asked.

Because you swore you'd never practice again.

The rest of the sentence hung in the air between us. Those were part of the things I wouldn't say aloud, and he knew better than to speak them into existence. Even now, we danced these careful steps around each other, cautious despite the lack of living flesh.

"She had kind eyes," I said, pouring over the book I'd pulled down from the shelf above the kitchen sink. The stepstool wobbled beneath me, one leg a hair too short. I didn't look down. Didn't have to. He was always there.

Danny, cool as fall breezes, bringing juniper and the translucent gray swirl of woodsmoke. He would forever be that crisp fall morning, heart a stuttering muscle I couldn't calm or restart, the distance growing between us in his eyes as he moved beyond my reach. He'd died there, hooked up to all those machines, the threat of early snow in the weather forecast that morning.

But when I'd finally come home, passed over our blue threshold, beneath my fading summer besom, he'd been waiting for me. Danny had remained with me since, a shade of himself but still somehow alive as ever. Never solid, never a man I could pull to me, wrap my arms around, but seeing his face and hearing his voice was enough. I would take him any way I could have him.

Ghost or spirit, husband or lover, my constant companion.

I'd asked him once why he'd come back, in the hours between three a.m. and first light, that in-between space that belonged to the writers and painters, the singers hearing secret songs, the ambrosia hour when anything is possible. His response had been simple, four words, *I made a promise.* We'd face what came after death together. A sworn blood oath given beneath a fading quilt, a pattern called wedding rings, fitting our new marriage, our new life —a thousand promises tying our souls together.

Emily had been full of promises too. The desperate kind born in the dark, staring at empty cradles and motionless rocking chairs, with the slide of headlights through the open nursery windows, the early morning hours dragging out as a grandfather clock ticked in the hall.

I'd seen it all so clearly when I took her hand.

I couldn't let anyone go back to an empty room like that.

"Kind eyes," he repeated.

"Exactly."

He came to stand below me, reaching out a steadying hand even though he couldn't stop me if I fell. Old habits, I guess. I had them too. I still stood up on tiptoe to kiss him in the mornings, made enough coffee for two, and bought two toothbrushes at the store when it came time to replace them. Living was like that, so hard to give up.

I met his eyes, finding a smile and knowing in his gaze, not reproach or disappointment. Not that I'd really expected either of those. But a small question had bubbled up, tiny as mustard seeds, to touch the surface of my mind the moment after I'd told Emily I would help her.

"I want to do it," I insisted. I tapped the open book, full of knowledge and hints of what might be possible. "I can figure it out, and I can do this."

He nodded, grin widening.

"What?" I asked, corners of my tips twitching, a smile curling into my cheeks.

"Nothing." He shook his head, one shoulder lifting in a shrug. "It's just nice to see you working at it again."

"I never really stopped." I closed the book with a snap and eased down from the stepstool, knees popping loudly. They didn't hurt so much as ache around the clock. All my joints did at this point, a dull throb that I'd grown accustomed to and come to expect.

"No, but you slowed down."

"Everything has slowed down."

The response was tart, and he chuckled.

I set the book on the table and turned to a cabinet. The door squeaked as it swung open, underlining his point about it being a while. Which it had. He was right. The last time I'd opened this door was when he'd been dying, pale in a bed, blood collecting beneath his skin, dark smudges beneath his eyes. I'd opened it and found nothing inside that could save him, nothing in me that could change the way the world was turning.

Three years? Almost four? Long enough, doubt shooting through me with the thought, would it all still be there, waiting for me to come back? Hello, remember me? Remember how I called your names and brought you shape and form? Remember the way the moon shines in a clear sky and hazes with humid spring nights? Remember the taste of fresh rosemary and chives, the orange-yellow nasturtiums tossed in salads and gracing kitchen tables? Do you remember blackberries warmed beneath bright suns?

Blackberries.

I stopped, holding myself so still that I stopped breathing, motionless so the thought wouldn't shy away. It was there, in the word and taste, the memory of summer sunshine and the buzz of insects.

"Blackberries," I said. The image was so clear in my mind—tart and sweet, fingers dark with blackberry juices, skin prickled from brambles.

"What?" he asked, coming around the kitchen table to look over my shoulder, inspecting the cupboard for brambles. "In here?"

"No, from along the tracks, the crossing down the way a bit. You know the one?"

Of course, he did. We'd picked blackberries from along the train tracks most of our married lives, a ritual of freezing and baking pies, cobbler with broken buttery crusts, the quick jam boiled on the stove and eaten the next morning, sticky lips and tangled kisses.

"I'll make the baby out of blackberries."

"And the sacrifice?"

My heart stuttered, the question shattering the elation. There would have to be a trade, an exchange. It was a balance, the right amount of give and take, and all petitions required a sacrifice. As above, so below, in this world and the next, I would have to even out the scales.

I shook my head, clearing the doubt, saving it for later.

"I don't know yet," I said, unwavering in my confidence. "But I know it'll work."

————

It was the right time of year for blackberries. If it hadn't been, I don't know what I would have done. Crab apples, maybe. Or late plums. Maybe I would have scoured farmers' markets for the last of the peaches or purchased bundles of sweet Vidalia onions. But it wouldn't have worked out so well; the spell wouldn't have held together without that balance of sharp and sweet, the prick of thorns and the snowy white of early blossoms. It could have only been blackberries for the baby. And she would be perfect, Emily's beautiful blackberry baby.

Early morning sunshine filtered through the stained glass of the front door, a ribbon of color that I passed through, touched and changed by color and light. *Remake me,* I whispered each time I bathed in the warmth, *make me new, and give me the strength to make this happen.*

Finally, armed with a plastic bucket and wearing a floppy gardening hat, I left the house. Danny stood on the porch watching, waving when I turned around to give him a smile and smiling in return as I moved out into the world.

The train crossing was less than a mile away, the

piercing whistles of passing locomotives a constant that had become background noise to my life, the rattling shake of chains and railcars. Blackberries grew all along the verges, right up to the gravel around the iron tracks, taller than I was in places, deep and thick right up into the pine trees that grew around our house.

This late in the season, birds and other animals would have picked off the easy fruit by now. Anything left would be deep inside the brambles, hidden by saw-edged leaves and twisted canes. I wore long sleeves and gloves to save myself the scratches, but I knew it didn't really matter. I'd come away with red welts anyway.

Blackberries never gave you anything for free.

———

I picked half a bucket of berries, reaching deep into the brambles, speaking softly to them, and taking my time. I spoke of longing and love, the things that brought people together and bound them tight to each other. I recalled sadness and disappointment, the way nights grew lonely when you were missing part of your heart, the things that might ease that ache and soothe the soul.

They shivered with my words, the air around me still, the woods thoughtful, considering each sentence carefully. Even the insects listened, the birds, the earth soaking it all up. Pressure built in my chest, and my fingers tingled, the shape of things to come shifting in the corner of my eye.

I would need candles and blood, a curl of new brambles, summer blackberries, last year's dead leaves, and water from the spring behind my house. The brambles and leaves were easy. I collected the water before I went inside. The candle came from a kitchen drawer, a remnant of a past birthday, and the blood came when I pricked my finger with a freshly sharpened paring knife.

I laid it all on the table, blood smeared on a white porcelain plate, candle lit and burning beside it. With a sigh, I sat and tried to clear my mind. Danny had given me the room, watched me come in with a bucket full of nature, and left the space quietly with an encouraging smile.

I popped a blackberry on my tongue, pressing it flat against the roof of my mouth, squeezing the juice out— summer heat, blackbirds squabbling over fruit, a rabbit hiding beneath trembling leaves. And a gift of sweetness, similar to the woman from the day before, given over without a second thought. She possessed that natural generosity. I'd seen it in her face. Emily's goodness had made me want to return it in kind.

A clock ticked somewhere in the house, a memory from another time, some other year, and then the front door opened. I sat straight up, insides fluttering as someone moved down the hall and into the kitchen. The woman, because that is what she chose to appear to me as, was tall and slim, red hair caught up in a crown of braids, gold arm bands on her upper arms, the dress she wore a rich amber.

"Hello, Antheia." I stood and smiled, relieved she'd answered, realizing now I'd been half convinced she wouldn't. I gestured at the table. "Would you like to sit?"

"This is all much more formal than usual, Gwen." Her voice was honey and cool water, bees and buzzing grasshoppers, a million tiny living things.

"Well, it's been a little while since we last talked," I said.

"But it's as if no time has passed at all."

Her smile warmed me. Having her here again in my house made me feel whole in a way I hadn't realized I'd been missing. She didn't sit, and I waited as she circled the kitchen, pausing to inspect the plants on the windowsill and the cuttings I had started on the counter. The seed packets I had picked out for fall were also sorted through with interest. Until finally, she turned her full attention to me.

"Tell me why you called, Gwen."

"I need to create something."

One eyebrow went up, green eyes intent on mine.

"A baby."

"For yourself?" she asked.

I shook my head. "No, for a woman I want to help. But I don't know where to start. Or rather, I do know where to start, but I don't know how."

"Blackberries?" Antheia picked up the wreath of brambles, turning it over in her hands thoughtfully. "An interesting choice. But I know nothing of children or the creation of them. I cannot help you."

With a sigh I sat, running a hand through my hair, the heaviness in my body weighing me down. I'd never considered she wouldn't be able to help me. I'd always turned to her, my patron goddess, and her support had transformed my life. She had always had every answer.

"Who do I ask?"

She came to me in a rustle of silk and cupped my chin, smoothing my hair back with her other hand. "Ask Evening. Maybe he'll be able to help." Her brows drew together as she studied my face. "You're already so much older. I forget sometimes how quickly humans fade."

"It all goes by so fast." I gave her a small smile, guilt coiling through me as I acknowledged how much time had passed since I'd spoken her name and invited her in. The sour bitterness of crabapples and fresh cranberries.

"It does," she agreed, stepping back. "I'll go out through

the back door. I would like to see what you've done with the garden this year."

"Antheia, I—"

Her smile stopped my words. "No, Gwen, no apologies. I just want to see the garden."

In a swish of silk and creak of floorboards, she was gone. I listened, waiting for the back door to open and close before I stood and peeked through the kitchen windows that faced the garden. It appeared empty. But it didn't feel empty.

With a sigh, I poured myself a glass of lemon tea and went out through the front door. If she'd suggested, it would only be a matter of time before Evening showed up.

———

Evening, the person not the time, arrived as the sun sank, the last warmth touching the stairs leading up to the porch, easing away as he climbed them. I offered whiskey or water, not surprised when he opted for apple juice and ice.

"Any news?" I asked.

We settled into the rocking chairs facing the front garden, pushing them into gentle motion with our feet, an offbeat rhythm as mine tilted forward and his back, switching places with a creak of solid oak. The scent of fresh-cut grass was in the air, the rattle of a train rolling by in the distance, and in my mouth, the contentment of sugary lemon tea and low voices.

"Of what kind?" he asked, glancing at me with dark eyes full of stars.

He'd never aged, always this middle-aged man with wild salt-and-pepper hair and an intense gaze, fine-boned and thin, ready to leap away. A heady moment caught between the end of the day and the start of the night, given shoulders to lift and legs to swing.

I shrugged. "Just curious. Wondering if there was anything new going on out there. I haven't left my place much lately."

"Oh, well. You know how it is. We're on the edge of Summer and Fall is around the corner. Those two have been in negotiations for weeks now. And honestly, Fall is weeks away yet. But she starts earlier and earlier each year, trying to get more time, pushing on Summer and Winter from both directions. I blame the pumpkin spice crowd."

He carried on with the local elemental gossip. Summer and Fall, a young woman and a middle-aged woman, arguing over space on the calendar. Winter, an older woman about my age, watched it all with laughter in her eyes. Spring didn't care. She was a child, playing her games and running all over the place now that her season of responsibility had passed.

The North Wind had come through, driving down a thunderstorm, rattling through and raising the hairs on the backs of everyone's necks. The Wood had stepped beyond his borders, one green foot into town, and dandelions had bloomed from every crack in the pavement. The personification of Rain had arrived and gone, flitting through before finding some other place more to her liking.

While I had been keeping my garden tidy and ignoring the world, it had all moved on without me. In a way, it was comforting. But it meant I was out of touch, grasping at loose ends, wondering if I still had it in myself to twist the strands of magic in the world together in such a way as to bring this gift into being.

There were so many doubts roiling through me, a tidal

wave, but there was one thing I knew in my gut. It had to be blackberries.

"Do you know where I could find whoever oversees the blackberry brambles beside the train tracks?"

He glanced at me and away, sipping apple juice and rocking the chair with a toe. "You might ask the Woods. He would know for sure but I don't know how you'd get a hold of him right now. He's out there wandering around, angry about that stand of trees that got flattened on the other side of town."

"Someone else then?"

"Summer."

"But she's dealing with Fall?"

"Yeah, well. Blackberries are a summer thing, right?"

"That's true." I stood up, back stiff, knees popping. "Come on inside for a minute. I have something for you."

I gave him a handful of blackberries to take with him, the purple-black fruit glossy in his dark hands. He thanked me, promised to send Summer my way, and left me to sift through the books stacked on the kitchen table.

———

A knock from the back door echoed through the house, polite and quick, in a hurry to be here and move on.

"Come on in!" I called from the kitchen, setting the dish down I was washing and reaching for a dish towel. "Door is open!"

Summer arrived in a rush, leaving the door open, heat and cicada song filling the house. She was petite and determined, browned by sunshine with a constellation of freckles across her face. She wore faded overalls and flowers spilled from every pocket, trailing and falling to the floor as she paced.

"Evening said you had a request?"

"Yes, I would like a baby. From blackberries."

Her laugh filled the air, a rushing wind, not unkind but surprised. "I've never heard of such a thing."

"No," I agreed. "I haven't either."

Tapping a finger against her lips she turned, eyes sliding over my kitchen, passing over me. She darted forward when she saw the cuttings on the counter.

"Oh! You're cultivating mock orange! How lovely!"

"Yeah." I smiled. "I haven't grown them before though. They're a new plant for me."

"They'll thrive," Summer insisted, laying a hand on each one, intense heat filling the kitchen. She turned to me then, matter-of-fact and all business as her season spun across the sky and filled my house. "And you need Orbona."

———

Emily called at the end of the week, voice small on the other end of the landline, cracking with distance and poor connection. But it wasn't time. I could sense the impatience, the desire, the want, but it was tempered, and I was grateful for her understanding. I felt it too, a tautness in my shoulders, tension coming up from the earth.

"Not yet," I said. "But soon."

———

I'd never petitioned the goddess of unborn children before, never had the need or really the desire. It had never even crossed my mind to start with her. We'd never had children, never wanted for them or missed them when they didn't come, so this was all new. I spoke hesitantly at first, wondering what she would think of a woman beyond childbearing years making this request. But as I went to pick blackberries and lit my candles at night, I explained.

I hoped it would be enough.

———

When we met, it was early morning in the brambles, a bucket in my hand and sun hat on my head. Red-winged blackbirds sang in the distance, sparrows squabbling in the canes, and already I was sweating through my thin cotton T-shirt.

"I've never heard of someone wanting a baby out of blackberries."

I turned to find a solemn woman studying me, gaze going beyond the layers of skin and muscle, looking into the essence of me, the outlines of my soul. I wonder what she saw. I hid nothing, not all of it good, not all of my life bad. A very human, human being. Flawed, regrets and mistakes, and all. But love and the true desire to help as well.

"I'm a gardener, and I wasn't sure who to ask at first," I admitted. "I've never wanted a baby before."

"But this one is for someone else?" A delicate eyebrow rose on her heart-shaped face, rich brown eyes flashing.

I nodded.

"Why would you do this for someone else? It's a big ask."

"I know."

"And you know this woman?"

"No. Not really."

"How do you know she'd take care of the child? Love it as her own?"

I opened my mouth but shut it. I couldn't know for sure. I didn't know her. But I knew what my heart felt, what my soul knew, what blood and bone and marrow said was true.

"You have to give me some credit," I said dryly. "I am a witch."

"A nonpracticing witch."

I laughed. "A witch is a witch, practicing or not."

She laughed with me. It had been a small test then. She'd pushed at a boundary to see if it was solid, if I was dedicated. It was, I was. Nothing had changed at all, it seemed. I was still as I had always been.

"Very well." She clapped her hands, light flashing as palms met, the air vibrating with the ringing of silver bells. "Babies from blackberries is an unusual request, but I'll grant it. It's enjoyable to be surprised after all these centuries. Novelty is priceless."

I held my breath, excitement shooting through me.

"Feed the brambles, talk to them, and always be honest. They'll give you what you want."

"Thank you," I said, letting the breath go with a smile.

"You will need to give them three things from the woman—items you can hold and bury. She will give up something else too, an unseen thing, but that's a price to be decided on between her and me. And you will be responsible for the blackberries as long as you live. You must continue to visit and feed them. You will be a protector and caretaker. You are in my service from now on."

I nodded. The space along the tracks, between iron rails and tall pine trees, would become a temple, a sacred space bridged by gravel and blackberry canes, bumblebees, and lazy heat. I would go willingly each day for the rest of my life for the gift she offered.

"I'll see you very soon," she promised and vanished between one heartbeat and the next.

———

Emily's voice vibrated with excitement, words tasting of ozone and sweet melon, when I asked her to bring me three offerings.

She carried a clipping of her hair tied with ribbon, a photograph of her mother holding a baby—a tiny Emily in a fluff of blue ruffles—with a smile like sunshine, and a sealed letter.

"Is this enough? Should I have brought something else?"

I shook my head. "No, this is perfect. Give me two weeks."

———

I buried Emily's hopes, her dream, deep in the earth and told the blackberries about her. How blue her eyes were, how kind her heart. And I brought nitrogen-rich fertilizers —coffee grounds, leaves, and grass clippings.

I came and talked to them, praising them, sharing stories of my life and how I'd come to be here with them now. I shared as much of myself as I could. If I wanted something so large from them then I needed to give them everything I could now.

When new blossoms began to sprout so late in the year, I knew my petition had been answered. They grew quickly, blooming and fruiting in a matter of days, bees buzzing from one white blossom to another, butterflies landing delicately, and other insects coming and going. I began to check several times a day, gauging how the fruit ripened, trying to guess when it all might come together.

I went early one morning before the sun broke over the horizon, the air a misty pink. I hummed as I went, the song something from our days of dancing in the kitchen and laughing over jelly glasses full of cheap wine. I'd been thinking about those things more and more as I wandered around the house and thought of life and death, birth and rebirth. What the woods would give me, what I would give away.

A willing sacrifice is still a sacrifice, still a hole in my body, a little bit less of me to walk the earth. But I was willing and able to do this for this woman. It didn't matter that she was a stranger, so unknown to me. In her story, in her face, I had seen aspects of myself, and that was enough.

Nearby a blackbird sang, greeting the dawn, calling awake the rest of the world. I liked this time of day best, when all things were possible, and it was all new. Each day a fresh start, each evening a chance to remember and sift through the day.

When I reached the train tracks, I knew.

———

My breath caught as the leaves rustled, something moving from deep within the bramble patch. Not a bird or rabbit, too small to be a deer or dog. I'd come every day for two weeks, an offering in the white plastic bucket, carrying away nothing but my own hope for the future and what it might hold. And now, maybe this would be the reward I'd been so desperate to receive.

A baby pushed through the low canes, hair black and shiny like a grackle, skin warmed and tan with sunshine, and blue eyes almost violet. A beautiful baby girl. She was bare as trees in winter, sprung out of the earth and blackberries with nothing but herself, and she looked to be about one. She stumbled as she walked, still new on her legs, still getting her feet right.

I held out my arms, scooping her up, laughter bubbling out of me, flowing over us, and then she began to laugh too. She placed two chubby hands on my cheeks, searching my face. I could taste the question, the blackberry bramble sweetness, and the needing to know. I answered as best I could.

"I'm not your momma. But you're going to meet her soon. You're going to love her, baby. She's been waiting for you for such a long time. Do you want to meet her?"

The child nodded.

"Good. Let's get you back to the house and cleaned up. You've got mud between your toes."

I settled her on my hip, leaving the bucket behind, telling her all about the woman who would be her mother.

———

"You got to let her go," he whispered.

"I never said I was going to keep her," I said, swiping at a tear on my cheek.

"I know," he murmured soothingly.

It was the tone that had always gotten under my skin when he could still breathe and make floorboards creak. Not patronizing exactly but reminding me that I knew better and had agreed to something already. I waved him away, plunging my hands back into the sink to scrub plates.

It had been a long time since I'd washed for two. And in a day, I would be back to washing for one.

"She'll be here tomorrow. Or the next day." I kept my gaze on the window, on the little girl running around on the lawn with a wand made from a stick and several long ribbons. She was already taller than she had been, a little older already, and I had no idea when she'd stop growing.

"I'm ready for the baby to go home."

———

I rocked her to sleep, cradled in my lap, the chair on the porch creaking and the night music coming on strong. She slept peacefully, hands balled up beneath her chin, thick eyelashes resting on browned cheeks. I could feel her heartbeat, it matched mine, joined as we were by magic, by the sacrifice I'd made for her.

This might be the last time I held a sleeping child. There had been so few in my life, never my own. That hadn't been planned, it had just worked out that way. Time had gotten away from us, me with my work and him with his studies. The two of us wandering around the house in slippers and robes, passing each other with air-blown kisses.

———

I almost felt his touch, the sweetness of it, the tenderness in flesh and bone. I think it was the memory. And I couldn't mourn all those years, I couldn't regret the things we hadn't done for the things we had. Our lives, my life, had been full and lovely, filled with perfect moments. I could let go of the child's hand and not be sad she wasn't staying. I could let go and still love her.

"She knows you love her," he whispered, a nothingness brushing across my ear, his voice reaching in to soothe the ache.

"You think so?" I smiled down at her face, gulping air, forcing the tears to stay where they were. Goodbyes, even planned and prepared for, were always so hard for me. I hated letting go.

"I do," he said, coming around to stand beside me, studying her perfect face with me. "You can tell by the way she looks at you. But she knows her mom is coming. You promised she would be here."

I nodded, knowing it was time, the right time, deep in my bones with that witchy sense of timing.

"Let's go meet your momma, baby girl."

The three of us went outside. I carried the baby into the yard, coming around the house until the driveaway came into view. Danny stuck to the front porch, a sentry waiting for my return. Emily was there, picking her way down the gravel just as she had been that first time, head down, watching where she was going. But this time, there wasn't that air of defeat and sadness hovering around her; today, she was wrapped in excitement, and I could taste late summer blackberries and mint, the coolness of well water. The way summer tasted when you sucked it in with your mouth open and eyes closed.

"Look who's coming," I said, voice soft, pressing my cheek to the top of her head. "It's your momma."

The baby wriggled in my arms, impatient to be put down, ready to meet her mother, ready for her life beyond my bubble to start. *Beginning.* It was singing in the air around us and tasted of honeysuckle and rain.

Emily was hurrying now, face alight with joy, tears collecting in her eyes.

"This is all you, baby." I set her down, steadying her, one hand on her shoulder. "You get to make the final choice, there's always a choice, but you can seal the magic, you can stay in this place if you want her as much as she wants you."

She took a step forward, distance growing between us, stretching out and filled in with my own mix of joy and sadness. This is what I'd wanted, what I'd worked my magic for, but it was bittersweet on the tongue. Then the baby was running to Emily, arms out, hair streaming behind her, running home to Momma.

The two came together in a tangle of tears and laughter, Emily on her knees and burying her face in the child's shoulder, touching her all over to see if she were real. Blackberry Baby laughed, a look of awe in her eyes as she placed tiny hands on her mother's face.

Are you real?

Is this you?

Are you mine?

"Thank you," Emily said, glancing up at me, eyes shifting back to the baby.

They couldn't take their eyes off each other as she stood, the baby on her hip, clinging to her, the child staring at her as if she'd never seen anything so beautiful in her life. Everything the world contained could not be as lovely as the woman cradling her now, professing love at first sight, promising the moon and stars in a single breath.

All of it for you, my darling.

I waved to them, smiling, the ache of it in my cheeks and behind my eyes. I was crying too, but happy tears. For them and what we'd brought into the world. For what she'd made space for and professed to love when it was only an idea, only a dream.

For her, love had been enough.

I hoped we would all find ourselves so lucky.

I didn't watch them walk away, didn't need to keep an eye out or make sure of anything. Emily had her now, the blackberry baby born of summer and sweet glossy fruit, love, and hope.

Danny was waiting for me, and I was ready to go home.

THE DEER WOMAN

I am silence and sharp things—shattered bone and broken branches, a high scream cut short. The trees are motionless, breathless as I am, listening, focused on the quiet now that the voice is gone.

I am here.

And I know your name.

———

Headlights knife through the night, a moonless darkness, infinite stars and endless cosmos overhead. The passenger door window is cool against my cheek, the car humming along the road, cutting through hours—this is time travel, nothing changing, everything moving. When we stop, I will have gone from starting point to destination with little thought or memory of what came between.

Here, with my face pressed to the glass and looking up, I can watch the stars and listen to the radio. I can ignore his anger and frustration. It'll pass. It will pass like this night, it will go on beyond this point, traveling through time as well.

Maybe it's as endless as everything above me. Maybe nothing will ever change.

The gun on the seat between us is compact. It's such a small thing. Something that I'd seen before, tucked in a kitchen drawer. *Honey, grab a pen out of the junk drawer in the kitchen.* That was the last time I saw it. If my hands were free, I'd grab it, and without hesitation, I would put it to his head—kill or be killed, eat or be eaten, do or die.

But we are past that point now. The zip ties are biting into me. My shoulders pulled back so tight, I'm a butterfly in the middle of being made ready for display. Soon the pin will plunge through me, stick me tight to a place I will never escape. I will be forever preserved when we reach the destination.

"You don't understand."

He's speaking. Telling me about his love, the bigness of it, the weight on his soul, the hurt I've caused by failing to live up to his expectations of me. *You.* Could have been. Should have been. Red flags flutter between each word, and now that I see them, I see them everywhere.

How we got from the apartment to the car is a blur. More time travel. I have simply gone from point to point, quickly approaching the end, and will have done nothing for myself. I have given tears, saltwater tracks down my cheeks, and a coffee-stained tooth. Blood as well; I have given that, and I know I will give more.

———

There is an after in the dirt, when my blood mixes in and it becomes mud, as the trees shiver and the woods hold their collective breath.

It is all silence now that my screams have been cut

short. I heard them go, knew in the moment that death had come for me, and I welcomed it, ready and willing, a lover trembling with desire.

But oblivion has refused me, leaving me wanting, gasping, hitching breaths filling my ears, thundering through my head. I am begging. I don't know who. I don't know what. I am simply pleading with the universe at large for release.

I plead for transformation.

———

Tears have slid across my temples, mingling with blood, more moisture for the earth. Maybe when the spring comes, flowers will curl up, spring into being from this spot, rising through my bones, forget-me-nots and poppies. I pray that I carry those seeds with me, that somehow, I've secreted them away all this time without realizing it. It is foolish, even as I think it, thoughts circling, incoherent and twisted with nonsense.

When the footsteps first break through the chaos in my head, I don't understand. But they grow louder, nearing until a woman steps into my line of sight. Part of a woman. She is beautiful from the waist up, small-breasted and nude, her skin a lovely dark shade that reminds me of polished stones and raven wings. Her other half is wild, the hindquarters of a black deer, hooves of obsidian, fur silken and reflective. She stares down at me with black eyes, no whites, no pupils, an endless unreadable gaze.

Get up.

Her voice is in my head. There without passing through my ears, without touching, vibrating through the delicate hairs in my ear canals. I can't get up. I can't feel my legs, I can't feel my hands. I shake my head, I believe I do, and inside I tell her, but I'm not really moving my head either. I'm not moving at all.

She kneels beside me, brushing matted hair from my face, smoothing the twist of pain from my forehead. She collects my tears, bringing them to her mouth, drop by drop, long black fingernails delicate as razors against my flesh.

Who were you before?
No one, nothing.
Who would you like to be?
Vengeance.

————

Her kiss is a gift. I accept ravenously.

————

Fire is in her skin, her touch molten—scorching, all-consuming. Fingers sink into my flesh, through muscle, until her hands wrap around the bones of my legs, remaking me, breaking me. If I could scream, I would. I would open up like a siren. I would shake the woods around me. I would hollow out the earth with my pain. She whispers to me, soothing, the voice in my head running through the pain, the two coming together, weaving, becoming one thing so that I don't know where the pain ends and her voice begins.

Soon. It will be over soon. You will be so beautiful when I am done.

It passes. Rebirth is not given without transformation, without the bite of pain, given in exchange to be something new. Shakily I stand, poised to run on delicate limbs, hooves strange and new but natural. I'm panting, drawing in air, exchanging oxygen and carbon dioxide, the trees breathe with me, my mirrors, and the woman before me smiles.

It's a gift. Take it. Collect your vengeance.

———

Beneath my new feet, unsteady on delicate limbs, the world is different. I am different, and yet this is how it should have always been. This is the woman I was meant to be.

Avenger. Siren. Destroyer.

Each unsteady step carries me forward, but I find balance and learn my new gait. By the time I am beyond the trees, I walk as if I've had hooves my entire life. Delicate deer legs. The transition from animal to human is smooth, natural. I am a partner to the woman in the wood, her mate.

———

How much time has passed? A day? A week? The season is new, no longer the cold of winter but spring. My bones were not the home of wildflowers. Instead, this new frame carries me, beating heart and fiery soul, forward and on without stopping.

The town is a shadow, unobserved as I pass, intent on one location.

The apartment is the same. Unchanged. Littered with empty beer cans, kitchen trash full of fast food wrappers, the dust of years on flat surfaces, and a hole in the bathroom wall gaping darkly.

I see it all.

There is a new woman on the sofa beside him watching television. Small. Shadows pool beneath her eyes, cigarette in one hand, a bruise on her cheek and on her wrist, where a hand had lingered with too much force. They sit together, close because he likes to keep us close, within striking distance because he dislikes the chase.

Blue light from a television reflects on the wall, my shadow extending from floor to ceiling. I move without touching doorknobs or passing through doors. I come into the room with a swirl of leaves and fallen stars. Somewhere, out of sight and from memory, a song begins to play. The music from the car has come with me, another form of time travel and magic, the last song.

Our song.

I smile, exposing sharpened teeth, hate and vengeance, sweet pleasure collecting in my belly, tense excitement and gluttonous hunger. There is no fear. I no longer feel that for this man. Or love. That has fallen away as well. I am glad to be free of both, shed like a skin, discarded and forgotten.

"William."

I speak his name, one word, but with it comes a thousand implications, every threat and promise he made.

I deliver on each one.

———

In two quick strides, I have overtaken him, pushing him down, face into the tan fibers of the carpet; stained and worn, my own DNA twisted in the roots, washed away but not gone.

He is soft with idleness, beer belly and balding head, soft hands. His shirt is worn, proclaiming loyalty to his guns. A mediocre man, a small man. Hazel eyes swivel from my face to my new legs, my beautiful hooves. I will show them to him, I will let him see them up close.

In a feverish madness of rage and joy, he dies beneath me. The girl in the apartment is watching—eyes round, pupils expanded into black holes, hand covering her mouth. The television is on, the murmur of Sunday sitcoms fading as we stare at each other.

"Will you take me too?" she whispers, trembling on the sofa, a woman who reminds me of myself, broken and reshaped by the hands of others, trapped in the sucking tar of existence.

I don't respond, can't find my voice or the ability in my body to shake or nod; muscles and tendons were not made for interaction with this poor thing. Vengeance has been delivered, justice in an elemental form, directly from the heavens to him, passing only through me, victim and killer in one.

I turn away. That is all I have to give to her. As soon as I do, she is forgotten, faded into the background, and I go back into the night, slick and shiny with blood, cheeks stretched with a grin I will relish for eternity.

———

I am seen as I pass through the outskirts of town; ragged humanity, peaceful lit houses, vestiges of commerce. A dog barks. A woman washing dishes at a warm kitchen window freezes. A couple walking arm in arm through the park stop in their tracks, mouths open, eyes wide. They are not for me.

But the man. The man is mine.

He leaves a bar, alcohol on his breath, mind fuzzy with

private frustrations, anger and resentment. He pisses himself as I linger, poised to pass him by but caught by certain knowledge, the inevitable rushing toward us both. We are connected. We are destined.

He knows; he can see his death in my face; he knows I will come for him too when the time is right. When I hear the screams of the woman he professes to love. But I cannot prevent the future, I can only avenge, and that knowledge and frustration will lead to brutal retribution.

I don't touch him. I can't touch him.

Yet.

I know there will be others. I can feel them moving through the world. But I have time.

Now, I need to find my heart. The place it now resides. The woman in the wood.

The Deer Woman.

———

Whatever humanity that had held on, lingering in the corners of my mind, evaporates as I cross the border between the cornfield at the edges of their world and the woods of mine. I am happy to leave it behind, abandon it to find something much more valuable beneath the trees.

When you are done, come home to me.

She had said, *come home.*

I go.

She is the only home I will ever need.

FIRE WATCH

I'd always loved fire, not in the habit of setting it, but being close to it, lighting bonfires in the summer and hearth fires in the winter. I'd never met wildfire, never seen it up close, and the idea terrified me, the destruction. But in that, there was rebirth, resurrection, and it made loving such a force of nature easy.

―――――

In my twenties, I spent a long time watching for fire, ready to report and prevent, high in an observation tower over acres of national forest with a radio in one hand and binoculars in the other, so alert and in tune. But not once did I have to make that call, not once did I see the telltale wisp of white smoke.

―――――

In my thirties, when Fire came to me, I let him inside, welcoming consumption.

———

That fall, I came down from my perch, headed home after rain had chased him away, cool winds coming to rustle reddening leaves. It was my last season in the watchtower. I'd opted for a desk job in an office, air-conditioned and heated, a pay raise with bitter coffee and ringing phones. An hour's drive from my cabin, which sat beyond the verges of civilization but near enough, I could pretend to be human if I wanted to.

Coming back to town felt strange after what had happened in the woods, like coming up for air after swimming with sharks, the swirl of water filling my ears and leaving me lonely with memory.

When spring rolled around, I felt the itch to go, revel in the new season, hike the back trails and see for myself if the observation tower had survived the winter. Instead, I assigned it to a new Forestry Service hire, showed him how the radio worked and wished him luck.

I wondered if he'd discover the same things in the woods that I had.

I wondered what happened to Fire.

———

It was late summer when I met my namesake, Holly, knocking on the door, carrying blueberry moonshine and still-warm pizza.

"Holly?" she asked, and when I nodded, she smiled and said, "I'm Holly too."

We stayed up late telling stories, and she introduced me to Spring, fierce and bright, with a laugh that pulled fresh growth from the violets in my kitchen window. Spring led

me to the Mississippi River and to gravely charming moun-
tains, bubbling brooks, and fallen stars.

I made room for Summer at my small table when she
came, had to because I'd promised Spring I would. Can't
have one and not the other, accepting the heat as it brought
longer days and clear nights filled with stars. Sometimes I
wondered why they came out of the woods, wandering
across my threshold, exposing rarely-seen faces.

These spirits and old world gods, personifications of
seasons and dreamlike figures of ancient myths. How had
they found me, only human Holly?

Maybe the trees told them, in the slow language of bark
and reaching limbs, roots seeking in the dark earth for
something better. Maybe the robins carried it with them,
barn swallows, red-tailed hawks, or those chatty crows
who can never keep silent and share it all, whatever it may
be, with the whole world.

Come meet the woman who can see you.

———

First, a deer that was not a deer, but all at once *the* deer, the
very first from which all came after. The buck's wide antlers
seemed heavy, yet he held them gracefully, tall and regal at
the edge of the clearing around the cabin. Behind him stood
a white doe with two spotted fawns, unreal in the
encroaching dark. But they came forward when I offered a
pail full of well water. They were bigger, even the babies, as
big as horses, and I kept my distance, watching from the
porch until they'd drunk their fill and left as quietly as
they'd arrived.

A late Frost came with the spring. Not Spring, the thing
that is also a person, but the green fresh start that is really

the new year coming around. But Frost wasn't the spiky cold figure from stories, neither handsome nor ugly, merely a man in need of a cup of tea and a moment by the fire. I expected melting water and fading and the feeling of cold coming into my house. But he spoke of craggy peaks and vegetable beds, keeping shaggy ponies and milking cows, hoping for rain in the summer and an easy winter for his fields. He farmed, he watched the stars wheel overhead and did his part in the changing Seasons.

They, of course, were bigger, larger than life, some so tall I'd tilt my head back to look into strange faces. I made soups and salads and roasted chickens and built towers of whipped cream and fresh berries, pouring wine or coffee. And in return, I heard the stories, the ones going all the way back, past the fragile human memory. Past history. Stories of vastness and change, stories of a world being built and formed into something that might one day become the place I lived.

And when I fell in love, head over heels and hopelessly, it was when Fire came to see me.

———

I was in my forties, not feeling it, just the ache in my back and twinges in my knees, well past the point of romance in my mind. But he'd heard of me, I'd become a story too.

The woman who lived alone in the wilderness, disconnected but connected in the right ways, the woman who saw things others could not, who remembered the forgotten things. At that point, I'd had almost ten years of strange and beautiful things crossing my threshold, talked and befriended giants and tidal waves, shared dinners with Seasons, and given relief to the first creatures.

Fire had kept away because he'd assumed he'd be unwelcome. Who liked to see destruction coming? Only a few, I guess, not many. But I'd been expecting him, knowing he'd come out of curiosity, because of rumor.

And his first words, hoarse from a throat that rarely spoke, said, "Would you like to take a walk with me?"

"Yes."

We went into the woods, following the dirt road that would eventually take us to civilization if we let it. It was the other side of noon, bright and warm and just right, the light filtering through clouds and the swaying branches of the trees.

"They talk about you. Do you know? You have the thing they all crave."

"What is that?"

"Acceptance."

I nodded, curious but unsure how to phrase it. But he must have sensed it.

"For what they are, without expectations, without forcing change."

Another nod, wondering why it would have been otherwise. They were as everything else, just as they were and should be. Even the Storms, a collection from large to small with voracious appetites and a love for whiskey and broken things. I wouldn't want them any other way.

"And you didn't believe it? What did you expect to find here?"

He glanced at me, tall enough and yet closer to my height, so I didn't have to tilt my head too much.

"I don't know. It seems too good to be true, a mortal woman who sees? Who accepts without comment or question?"

I laughed. "Of course, I ask questions. Millions! I just

don't always get answers. Or I do, but I can't understand them. No one is ever willing to explain."

"Ask me anything."

———

How do you tell a love story spanning over years? The kind that builds so slowly you don't realize you're a part of it until it's already happened and somehow in the middle?

We found a routine, and when we kissed, I kissed him first, it was just right. A comfortable fit, as my mom would have said, and I just knew this was it. It didn't take me long to make up my mind and make room for him in my life.

I had to smile at that, a woman building a life with Fire, doing all the mundane things while the supernatural happened out of sight. We split chores and took turns cooking, we read and made love, we gardened and split logs for the hearth.

During the day, I spent my time at work, into town on the tired old tires of my truck, putting in hours at the forestry headquarters, behind a desk and computer, tip-tapping away and answering the phone. It was an hour's drive from my front porch and back, but I wouldn't have lived any closer. And I just shrugged when people asked if I was lonely up there all by myself.

"Don't you get lonely? Isn't it cold?"

"I've got a fire to keep me warm."

———

And he'd be there, waiting in the sunshine, with my name in his mouth.

———

After a decade, he became domesticated, my Fire. He would leave and come home again, bring flowers from distant places, bring maple syrup, and, *once*, crimson silk pajamas. After dinner and time spent with books, he would crawl into our bed, burrow beneath several quilts and too many pillows, and we would laugh and whisper into the night.

And when he said he loved me, I knew it was the truest thing.

———

It ends.

All of it.

Always.

Sometimes it is happily ever after, sometimes bitter because not everything can be easy or sweet. But mine was painless, mostly because they wished it for me, made me a place without pain, without the biting sorrow of letting go. A sudden and fierce heart attack, seized and tensed and seemingly infinite.

When I woke—because my eyes opened and what else could it be?—I was not alone. He waited, waited as if the end of the world couldn't stop him, waited as if I'd only ever been the one. And I knew, somehow, all those years, I'd been waiting too.

"And this is after," he said, holding out a hand for me to take, pulling me to my feet in front of a house that looked very much like our own. "If you wish it, if you want me, this is what comes after."

I turned with him to look at the cabin, the wide porch filled with potted plants, moss growing on shingles, the warm yellow glow behind the windows, and the open door. Overhead a million and one stars sparkled, a moon lowering in the sky, and at the edges of the world, a hint of dawn.

"I would never want anything else," I said.

A truth sharper than anything that had come before, as hard as love.

We walked toward the house, arm in arm, and I didn't have to turn to look into the trees to know they were all there; the Seasons, spirits of rivers and stones. I could feel their joy, their acceptance of me, I could feel them as part of me, and I knew I was now a part of them.

"I made dinner," Fire said, leading me up the porch and across the threshold. "I burned the chicken, but the mashed potatoes should be okay.

THE BLACK CAT
PART ONE: DOLLHOUSE

June brought summer and a black cat. Not the kind you buy at the fireworks stand as you prepare for the Fourth of July —that fearsome face and open maw, red eyes, white fangs. The black cat that came into my life was small and mild, willing enough to be held and petted, carried around in the crook of my arm as I moved between the playhouse in the backyard to the dollhouse in my bedroom. One life-sized, the other a miniature; my interior and outer worlds.

Onyx, as sleek and beautiful as the gemstone, green eyes alert and focused. I don't remember where he came from that summer. He was there as if he'd always been there, a bowl of kibble in the kitchen and a litter box in the garage. I'd never asked for a pet, and my mother hadn't inquired if I wanted one. Yet our lives were suddenly filled with the can opener whirring and his matching purr, the black body moving through the house at night, coming to lie at the foot of my bed when I slept.

He was my shadow, a companion through the hot days,

a silent playmate as I served invisible tea in plastic cups. Once he let me put him in a pink ruffled baby doll dress, ears laid back, tail twitching, a time bomb tick-tick-ticking.

At night I would stand at the back door, calling his name, my mother calling mine, our voices blurring into one as bedtime was announced.

"Onyx!"

"Maria!"

"It's time for bed!"

The backyard was a tangle of plants, the forgotten space of a previous gardener, shrubs and flowering trees, paths that wound beneath and through it all. My mother had rented the house for this garden, a magical place for a little girl to spend her afternoons. At night, filled with the rustle of nocturnal creatures, it was something else. I didn't like to be outside when the sun went down. I could feel how small I was out there, under the stars, with nothing around or above my head. I kept my feet on the cement step, one hand on the door frame, leaning out, calling until I thought he'd never come.

Then Onyx would appear, trotting smoothly out of the darkness, into the yellow glow thrown by the porch light beside the door.

A cat.

A small black cat.

Nothing more.

———

The doll was blonde, hair an unnatural shade, with pink lips and blue eyeshadow. Sometimes when my mother went out, which was rare, she wore the same color—

frosted and cool-toned, bringing out the azure in her green eyes.

Once I'd snuck into her room while a babysitter talked on the phone, pressed a single finger into the pan of color, and swiped it across my eyelids. I admired myself in her dressing table mirror, the way I suddenly looked so adult, sophisticated, and worldly. I forgot to wipe it away before my mother returned. I was half-asleep in my room when I felt the cold washcloth, panicking awake as she gently removed the makeup—rich, heavy perfume filling the air.

I wasn't told to keep out of it, not scolded or warned. She brought me my own the next day.

"You're too young to wear makeup, Maria. But you can play with it as much as you like at home."

From then on, I'd swipe shimmery blue across my face, Onyx watching as I did. Once I added some to his face, dropping a kiss on his soft fur. He washed it off as soon as I pulled away, tail twitching, back turned to me. I added it only to my dolls after that, their faces faintly blue and sparkling, as they went about their lives in the pink doll-house in the corner of my bedroom.

Three floors and an elevator, cardboard walls covered in stickers to make it appear as if the rooms were filled with furniture and a kitchen. I had pink plastic beds, a table and chairs, a bathtub that I filled carefully with water and bubbles, dolls stripping down to soak and read the carefully folded construction paper books I made. I mimicked my mother. The way I wanted to be when I grew up, when I could sip a golden drink from a cup shaped like a tulip and read books where handsome men embraced women with flowing hair and beautiful dresses.

Onyx stayed close, watching the movement of my hands intently, basking in the sun coming through the window, caught in warmth and dust motes. Sometimes I would prop a doll up against his side, pretend that he played with me, that he was a wild beast tamed and loved by a beautiful woman.

A panther as calm as a house cat, something wild domesticated.

———

A color I had no name for—deep and rich, vibrant and dark. Reminding me of scraped knees and paper cuts, the quick flash of a needle at the doctor. But not a color I expected here, in the shadowy hall, in my house in the middle of a hot Sunday afternoon. Buzzing filled my head, my ears thrummed, and I waved my arms around to brush the noise away. Sweat prickled along my forehead, my scalp itching.

I hesitated, pulled forward—the open door, the red trail leading into the space beyond, out of sight, into my bedroom.

The house was quiet. My mother was outside talking to the older couple across the street. Her name was Maria too. So many of us, wandering out in the world, connected by the sound of five letters. I thought about that, thousands of girls, like and unlike me. I thought of that instead of the blood in the hall. I thought of other little girls out in the sunshine, at the beach or riding their bikes down a street.

I would pretend I was another little girl.

A collection of droplets, a few here, a few there. Grouping together as if they were lonely, coming together to keep each other company. It wasn't much blood. Not really. But enough. Enough for me to know that something wasn't right. Enough for me to wonder why my mother hadn't seen it already.

I stood in the doorway of my room, going over each piece, looking for the out-of-place thing. The window blinds were open, pulled to the top, the glass covered in painted plastic sun catchers—flowers and watery paint—the sun shining through them to cast multicolored patches of light across my bed, the carpet littered with toys, and the dollhouse.

Struggling for breath, I gasped, unsure, not knowing, but feeling the wrongness of it all. An unnameable thing. A thing. In my bedroom. Where I slept. I turned to my bed, the darkness beneath it, so cool and complete, a wasteland beneath my box springs.

Anything could be under there.

But the blood led to the dollhouse. It stood between the window and the bed, the front turned to me, the facade printed to look like a real house. Pink brick. Bright green rose bushes. Windows tinted light blue, white reflections painted on them. Vibrant, unreal.

I crept forward, pulled, unable to turn away.

The sun warm on my skin, the carpet tinged yellow and blue beneath my feet, the sound of a lawnmower starting up in the distance as I came around to look at the inside. I stood motionless, going over the interior. All of it so familiar, a known structure, a known place.

The dolls were gone. In their place, sitting in chairs at the table and lying on the bed, were mice. Brown. Small. Long tails. Pink hands and feet. Black eyes open. Some looked whole, untouched, as if they'd come out of the walls to play house and gotten caught—frozen, fearful. Others had puncture wounds, fur bloody, a deflated quality to their bodies as if air were leaking out like it would from a balloon.

The mouse on the bed was the bloodiest. Throat ripped

wide, pale raw flesh exposed. The creature's head was almost detached. If I reached out, if I touched it, it would roll away, fall out of the house. My hand twitched, skin crawling. It would be soft. Almost no sound when it hit the floor, blood seeping into the carpet fibers.

Onyx appeared, rubbing against my legs, purring.

I ran from the room, panting, chest tight, leaving him behind. Out through the front door, flying down the steps and across the lawn to where my mother was laughing. Laughing as if my room weren't full of dead things.

"Mom! Mom!"

She turned to me, still smiling, holding out an arm so I could squeeze in close, press myself to her hip, feel her arm settle over my shoulders.

"You have to come see."

The neighbors chuckled, the other Maria sharing a look with her husband, a glance as if they knew what I was talking about.

"You go on in. We'll catch up later," said the other Maria. "Looks like she's got something important to share."

I nodded, swallowing.

"What is it, baby?" she asked, following me, a half smile lingering.

"You just have to see."

I didn't want to tell her. I didn't know what to say, how to explain.

Air conditioning hit us as we came through the front door, the house dim, blinds and curtains pulled over the windows. I hesitated in the entryway, on the tile, searching for more blood.

"Maria," my mother said, voice hardening, an edge of worry creeping in. "What's going on?"

I shook my head, taking her hand and guiding her

toward my room. She stopped in the hall, seeing the red droplets. Frowning, forehead wrinkling, brows coming together, she moved me aside, dropping my hand to hurry ahead.

I knew what she would see. The room a rainbow of color, the pink dollhouse, the dark wet spots, the mice. The hall seemed so quiet and dark compared to that space, a reprieve, a safe space. I wanted to stay here, to put off seeing what I knew to be true, the growing horror of it sneaking up behind me, great clawed hands reaching, ready to take me gently by the shoulders.

"Maria," my mother said. Invisible from where I stood, a figment, my name coming from a place I couldn't see. "Come here."

Stepping forward, shoulders back, I entered the room. There was nothing I could say, nothing to explain; she had seen everything I had, she would understand why I'd come running out of the house, desperate to show her something that shouldn't be there.

"Baby, I'm so sorry." She held out her hand, inviting me to cross the distance between us. "Onyx must have brought this in. Sometimes cats do that."

I didn't look down, didn't want to see all those dead mice sleeping and sitting—pretend dinners and sweet dreams. She seemed so casual, her words soft, nothing anxious or scared. Not the emotions I'd been expecting at all.

"You know," she said, taking my hand. "Cats usually bring you things because they love you and think you're unable to take care of yourself. That you're not grown-up enough yet to hunt."

"Because they love you?"

She nodded. "Yeah. He's brought you lunch."

"Lunch?"

"I'll get a bag and get it cleaned up. It'll just take a moment, and then it will all be good as new."

A bag? Would that be enough for all of those tiny bodies, the blood all over the printed cardboard and plastic? I sucked in a deep breath, pulling it into my lungs, holding it, my cheeks puffed out, and looked down.

A single mouse. Just the one. Bloody but whole, no missing limbs, the fur wet and matted. It was on the bottom floor of the house. Not in a chair. Not in a bed. Just lying there, as if it had been casually dropped—an offering, a gift.

I jumped as something brushed against my leg. Looking down at Onyx as he turned to brush against me again, arching his back, soft fur to bare skin. Soft, so soft. His purr filled the room, vibrating, and he squinted his green eyes as he looked up at me, something like a smile on his cat face.

I love you.

NIGHTMARE
PART TWO

The summer days were longer, stretching out, worn thin in places, transparent in the heat. I didn't play with the dollhouse again. My mother had been right, and she'd made it good as new. But still. Still. I didn't look beyond that word, refusing to pull what I felt into the light, into the direct rays of a summer sun.

I spent more time outside riding my bike down our hill, legs out, pedals spinning, tempted but not daring enough to let go of the handlebars and fly like the other kids on the street. I'd told Samantha—the girl up the street and a friend in the way that neighborhood kids are friends without being close—about the mouse, just the one, no more, and her face had crinkled up, a piece of paper wadded tight. Gross. So I didn't mention it again.

I would come home as the night closed in, sweaty and smiling, happy to have spent the day under the cloudless sky. Onyx would be waiting on the front porch, perfectly still, eyes intent, tail wrapped around his feet. He was always there, the first person to greet me when I came home, ready with a meow.

The rest of the time he came and went as he pleased. My mother or I would open the sliding glass door for him—in and out, out and in. He didn't bring me another mouse. Maybe he'd been disappointed when I hadn't eaten it, watching my mother pick it up in a washcloth and throw it in a bag, drop it in the garbage bin outside. Such a waste.

He sat and watched us eat dinner at the kitchen table. Salad. Hamburger and noodles. Baked chicken. Tacos. A rotation of things that never included something wild being brought in for dinner. Mice never graced our shatter-proof plates.

In the evenings, he sat on my mother's lap, the blue light of the television washing over our faces. Purring, eyes closed, he would reach out one paw to me, touching whatever was closest, hand or knee. He was always happiest when he could touch us both at the same time.

"All right," my mother said. "Time to get ready for bed. Brush your teeth and put your pajamas on. We'll read a couple of chapters tonight."

I nodded, hurrying to the bathroom, and slathered my toothbrush with bubblegum-flavored toothpaste. None of my other friends were read to at night, grown out of the bedtime story at the age of ten. But my mother continued, the reading level of the books improving as I got older. We'd long ago surpassed simple chapter books. We'd worked our way through *The Hobbit* and *The Lord of the Rings*. Now we were reading the Narnia books— full of magic wardrobes and lions, ships shaped like dragons, and dying planets.

Our routine was for me to start first. I'd read until I got tired, passing the book to her. Sometimes we had to reread because I fell asleep as she read. But I didn't mind. I liked the evenings propped up together in my bed beneath the quilt, the bedside table light on, the nightlight across the room glowing. Onyx joined us, inching his way up, squeezing between us, and purring gently.

I would fall asleep to the sound of my mother's voice.

————

I couldn't breathe.

A weight on my chest, so heavy. My ribs creaking beneath the pressure, heart throbbing. I was being crushed, pushed through the mattress, down into the foundation of the house, past concrete, into the cold hard earth.

Scream.

I tried. I wanted to. It lodged in my throat. Opening my eyes, coming out of the dream, the pressure on my chest didn't ease, didn't fade. It was just as heavy, just as present. My room was black, the nightlight burned out, no light on in the hall or the kitchen.

My mother always left a light on for me.

I couldn't move my arms or legs. My lips refused to part. An unbearable weight. I wasn't going to survive this. Sunshine was over for me. Fruity cereal in the mornings at the kitchen table. Exploring the creek behind our house. Giant frogs and lightning bugs. Blue eyeshadow. My mother's warmth, the way she hugged me tight, kissing the top of my head.

It was all gone.

The purr started then, sinking into muscle and bone, filling me. The weight on my chest eased slightly, enough so that I gasped, pulling in air. Onyx. I knew him now, recognized him in the dark. But he didn't move. He continued to sit on me, purring in the dark, an endless thrumming in my head.

I felt a paw, the tips of claws in the softness, as he

touched my face. Gently, tenderly. And then he retreated, lifting off my chest completely, and I felt his weight on the bed beside me, the thump he made as he left it, jumping off the mattress and landing on the floor. I listened, the purr continuing, retreating down the hall.

LOCKET
PART THREE

I was twelve when a new family moved in on our street. A girl my age, my grade. Diana. Named after a princess, a dead woman, but looking nothing like her. This girl had white-blonde hair, cut short in a sharp bob, and eyes so blue it hurt to look into them.

We'd walked home together, talking about the gym teacher we shared, the kids in our separate homerooms. A tentative friendship, something fresh to go along with the new school year—new clothes, white sneakers. I was still feeling it out, trying to navigate my way into it.

At my house, while my mother worked toward the end of her day, we ate cappuccino chocolate ice cream out of blue bowls and watched the last thirty minutes of daytime television—heavily made-up women and dramatic lighting, music over it all, clinging like perfume.

"Got a bathroom?"

"Sure." I pointed with my spoon. "Down the hall and on the right."

She'd excused herself, going back to the restroom, leaving me to scrape out the last few pieces of chocolate clinging to the side of my blue bowl. Then she was back, in a hurry to leave, backpack over a shoulder and already at the front door.

"I'll see you tomorrow, okay?" I smiled at her, question and declaration all in one.

"Yeah, okay."

After putting our bowls in the sink and shaking cat kibble into Onyx's red dish, I wandered back to my room. I had homework to do. Math. Spelling. But I wanted to lay on my bed with a book by Patricia C. Wrede more than I wanted to expand myself in other directions. Dragons, a princess, and talking cats were better companions.

The box on my dresser was open. Simple, carved wood, scrolls, and almost flowers, something that must have been mass-produced but precious to me. A place to keep the things I valued, treasures secreted away, hoarded for a day I would need them.

My stomach sank. It had been picked through, gone over, junk and debris to the searcher, finding very little worth taking. A bracelet. A pair of snap-on shimmery earrings made of glass. A gold-plated heart-shaped locket.

"No, no, no!"

I dumped the contents on the floor, sinking to my knees and spreading it all out. I had to be sure. I could have missed the glitter, a hint of gold, a reflection of light. Tears pooled in my eyes and fell, a sob coming up from my gut. It was more than the stolen items. A loss. Friendship offered with one hand and taken away with another.

Snot touched my upper lip, the room blurry around me, and I let out a howl of grief. No one else was here. My mom wouldn't ask questions, wouldn't peel away the Band-Aid to poke at the rawness of this wound. I couldn't face telling her about the missing locket, a Christmas gift, our photos together inside.

A soft body touched me, small and silky, Onyx making a questioning sound. I jumped, startled, blinking tears away to see him clearly. He looked from my face to the pile in front of me, my hands balled into the carpet.

"Oh, Onyx." I sobbed, picking him up and burying my face in his fur. "Diana took the locket Momma gave me."

He began to purr, warm in my arms, the sound growing, filling my head, and sinking into my bones. I wanted to go back to ice cream and walks home, to someone I'd thought was my friend.

———

More was gone than just the locket. She'd stolen a bracelet —a purple circle, glitter trapped in clear plastic, large enough that it would slip off if I wasn't paying attention. Pay attention. And two sparkly clip-on earrings. I didn't tell my mom. I didn't want her to know that I'd lost the locket after she'd told me how important it was to hold on to.

The next morning, quiet over breakfast, I pretended to be sick. My stomach hurt. But it wasn't much of a lie. My mom, in a hurry to get to the office on time, promised she'd call to check on me. There were cartoons and cereal until the quiet afternoon with Onyx on the sofa beside me. He lapped up the leftover milk, licking his whiskers, cleaning a paw.

When it was time, I got dressed quickly, hurrying to beat the bus, fast walking to Diana's house—Diana the thief, Diana the backstabber. Onyx followed but somewhere along the way, I lost him, or he lost me, and when I reached her backyard—silver chain-link fence, green garbage cans, tan siding, and red brick—I was alone.

I didn't have to wait long, jittery with expectation. She came around the corner of the house, swinging a yellow backpack and humming, the purple bracelet flashing on her wrist. When she saw me, she stopped, face reddening. I held out my hand, palm up, waiting.

"You took my locket, Diana. I want it back."

"I didn't take anything from you."

I began to shake, hurt and wounded, heart pounding, tears threatening.

"You were in my room!"

"I don't know what you're talking about." A sneer on her face, denial and a lie, determined to stick to it all.

Diana tried to move past me. I blocked the gate, holding onto it, trying to stop her from walking away. I gripped the chain-link fence, desperate, my cheeks wet with tears.

"Get out of the way!"

"I want my locket!" Begging, pleading, wishing so hard my heart hurt. I wanted the necklace back. I wanted to pretend this hadn't happened. "I thought you were my friend."

"You're stupid, Maria! You're stupid and I hate you!"

"Please, Diana!"

"Get out of the way!"

Diana kicked me, white sneaker against my bare leg, tearing the skin, blood welling up. I faltered, fell away, the chain links rattling, the gate unguarded. She ran past me and into her house, taking the purple bracelet with her.

———

The phone in the kitchen rang—beige plastic, extra-long spiral cord.

"Maria, would you get that please?"

I jumped up from the sofa, abandoning Saturday morning cartoons, and ran to the phone, catching it mid-ring.

"Hello?"

"Hello?" An echo of greeting but somber, heavy across the buzzing line. "Is this Maria?"

I made an affirmative noise.

"Can I talk to your mom, honey?"

"Sure," I said, turning to my mom at the sink elbow deep in soapy dishes, and held out the phone. "It's for you."

With a sigh, she wiped her hands and took it. "Hello? Yes. Oh! Annette, hi. I didn't recognize your voice for a second. What's going on?"

I watched her face fall, the friendliness and warmth dropping, the somberness of the voice on the other end of the line overtaking her, changing her. My mom's eyes fell on me, an unreadable expression, one never seen before. Something like fear, horror, terrible sadness.

"Hold on just a second," she said, covering the mouthpiece with a hand. "Go play in the backyard for a little bit, okay?"

———

It was in the playhouse waiting for me. My shin still scabbed and bruised from Diana's tough sneakers, the kick with so much anger behind it. I could still feel the chainlink fence in my hands, desperation in my heart. How fragile my idea of friendship was. How easily it proved false.

I'd come to hide, clutching a book and glass of water,

not minding if the space was filled with spiders. No door. Simple square for windows. A child-size table and chairs. Dim in the back, the light not reaching, not touching the deep corners—rough wooden walls, weatherworn.

A sparkle on the table caught my eye. A beacon. A silent screaming object.

I paused, watching it as if it could move, as if legs might sprout and it would scuttle away. *Move.* Because if it moved, that meant it wasn't real. A trick of the light. A game played by shadows. A shard of nightmare coming into the day, something to blink away, rub from my eyes like sleep.

An ear. Small. Pale. A shiny clip-on earring attached.

My earring.

Cicadas sang, droning love songs into the air. The sun on my back, hot through thin cotton. The book in my hand was light, the cover glossy, the pages within the recycled brown color of cheap paper. No shoes. I was half in, half out, my toes on the bare boards of the floor, heels in the dirt outside.

I was between two places and holding on to everything outside the pretend house for all I was worth.

But it was inevitable that I would go inside. It was coming and I couldn't stop it.

So I stepped forward to meet it.

The other earring was there too. The purple bracelet and gold locket. I didn't reach for them, I didn't touch them. But I wanted to. I wanted to know if the photos of my mother and I were still inside, our photographed faces pressed together, kissing in the closed-off darkness of the metal heart.

I licked my lips, mouth dry, forgetting the water in my hand, the book. And I knew I wasn't alone. It wasn't there the moment before, the area all mine, mine to scream and cry in without a witness. But I could feel it waiting, watching.

"Maria!"

The glass shattered as it hit the ground, and I took a stumbling step back. Several pieces of glass lodged in the bottoms of my feet, and I screamed, falling back on my butt, the book flying away. The pain intense. I could hear my mom running, voice high, as blood seeped into the dirt, my feet on fire.

Through tears, I saw something shift in the dim interior of the playhouse.

––––––

Later, my mom brought the jewelry inside and returned it to the cheap box on my dresser. She didn't ask why it was there. It didn't matter. What mattered were the cuts in the soles of my feet—how soon they might heal, how I would go to school, and if she could get the time off work to take care of me.

I wanted to ask her about the ear. I wanted to know if she saw the blood, the small pale piece of human flesh in the playhouse, in our back garden, in our lives. Did she remove one sparkling earring, clean it off, and put it back?

Instead, she told me about the phone call, voice serious, concerned eyes searching my face. Diana went missing. It was her mother on the phone, the worried Annette. The police wanted any information about the last time she was seen. I swallowed the lump in my throat, terrible certainty filling me. My mouth began to water, nausea setting in.

"Diana went missing after school yesterday. Have you seen her? Her mom said she was here a few days ago, she said you guys watched some tv and ate ice cream. Have you seen her since then?"

The ear. The false glittering earring. The shadow moving in the corner.

"No."

DOCTOR
PART FOUR

A blank room like a canvas, ready for whatever might happen, whatever it might contain. Anything could happen in a room like this. Beneath me, paper crinkled, bleached white, sterile. I looked down at my nails, chewed down to the quick, cuticles raw, and I had to stop myself from picking at them, peeling tiny strips of skin away; the satisfaction it brought, the small point of pain—forgetfulness, distraction.

Beyond the door, I could hear the whispered conversation; my mother's voice tense but rising, the doctor a monotone calm. This wasn't my regular doctor, the one I went to for rashes and colds, her office was brightly colored; bright blue and green halls, the rooms I waited in purple and red, flowers and artwork done by other kids. I'd given her a drawing once, the two of us together, with her handing me a Band-Aid. It had still been there on my last visit.

Doctor Richardson had suggested my mom take me here. A card handed over gripped tight, my mom's hand trembling; red nails, a gold ring with a pale green sparkling stone.

Doctor Alvarez, a man with very serious eyes and no hair, asked me questions while my mom filled out stacks of paperwork. Yes and no questions, little dots she filled in with a pencil, a focused, determined expression on her face.

"Do you have nightmares?"

"Do you feel anxious? Worried?"

The questions went on, and I answered as best I could. A little hesitant, not wanting to give away too much. I needed to keep myself pulled in tight, elbows close to my body, hands clasped in my lap, ankles crossed.

I didn't tell him about the pale pink ear, the bloody mice. The weight on my chest in the middle of a pitch-black night.

It was the information he was after. The reason my mom had brought me here without knowing it. She thought it was Diana. Stress. Fear. *What if?*

"A girl on our street went missing last week, a friend. They haven't found her. And there's something wrong with Maria. She jumps a mile high if I startle her. I know it doesn't seem like much. I know it. But I know my daughter, something has changed."

Grief. Shock. These were the reasons she was given, a book to teach us both coping mechanisms, the suggestion of medication. Pills in a transparent orange bottle, white safety cap, with my name in harsh black letters on the label; warnings, directions. And a list of names of someone I could talk to once a week.

The car ride home was quiet. I glanced at her once, tall enough to sit in the front seat now, the car behind us long and hollow. I wished I'd sat in the back, behind her, so I wouldn't have to look at her, watching the world roll by, imagining a black cat racing us, keeping pace on the shoulder of the highway. But her silence, the way it spread out between us, made it impossible to ignore.

———

"You know you can talk to me, baby? You know that, right?"

I nodded. "Yeah, of course."

"Anything you need, I'll help you with. I'll listen, it doesn't matter what time it is or where. I'll be there for you. Always."

"I know. I love you, Mom."

"Okay," she said, pulling me into a tight hug. Squeezing me, she buried her head in my shoulder, holding onto me as if she could keep whatever haunted me away.

Behind her, walking out of the kitchen, Onyx watched us with curious green eyes.

BIRDS
PART FIVE

There is a cliché about lonely children. Everything happens to them; horrors and adventures, the glint of destiny on steel, a kiss that changes the world. I was that child without the call to something greater. I played with dolls until I was too old, kept books close, walked with my eyes down through hallways filled with lockers and voices raised to reach the ceiling.

The few friends I had seemed to fade away over time. There were no sleepovers and gossip, no painted nails while names were tossed around, no crushes and broken hearts exchanged. The boyfriends I picked up were never anyone I brought home to meet my mother. Kisses in parked cars, sweaty hands, fumbling, tumbling, coming together and falling apart.

After it all, at the end of days or nights, months or years, Onyx waited.

How long did I know I lived with a monster? My monster? I'd heard stories about creatures living beneath beds, inhabiting closets and small dark spaces. The boogeyman, a myth, a legend. It took a long time to admit it to myself, in the quiet of my mind, in a place filled with sunshine and silence. I never said it out loud. My mom never believed in monsters. Not real. Not a part of our reality. But even as small as I was then, I knew that didn't mean we weren't a part of theirs.

I carried that thought, that idea, with me into adulthood.

And Onyx followed me there.

Not all childhoods are magical. Sometimes, as you grow up—up and up until there is nowhere else for you to go but out of the house, out into the world—you look back and see the flaws.

It was a single-parent house, my mother working late into the evenings, as I let myself in the house after school, remembering to set the frozen chicken on the counter to thaw. I did homework at the kitchen table alone, watched television, and read. Sat out in the backyard, watching the night approach, stars and lightning bugs filling the sky, waiting for the bolt on the front door to turn, for Mom to call out to me.

"Maria!"

I still hear her voice.

Onyx was there when she passed, splitting his time between my tiny apartment in town and my mother's house. I would drop him off for long weekends or stretches during the week. A kind of joint custody that he seemed to prefer.

At first, I'd taken him with me. But he sat at the door and howled, inconsolable, until he saw her again. She said after a few days with her, he did the same thing at her house. And when she'd been in the hospital and he'd yowled for her, I asked the nurse if I could bring him to visit. She'd looked at me strangely but nodded. I carried him up in my arms, calm and patient.

When she passed, I was holding her hand and Onyx was purring.

———

Orphan.

All alone in the world. It felt strange to know I'd never see my mom again, never hold her hand or eat dinners cooked with love—favorite things, comfort foods. But not really alone. Onyx was there too.

How long do cats live? Living their nine lives, separate from you as they go out into the world, beyond the open door, passing by you without a backward glance. Did they still belong to you, then? I sometimes wondered if other people left food on back porches or ran their hands along his back to scratch the base of his tail. But he always came back to me, sitting close, reaching out to touch me with one paw to let me know I belonged to him.

He went out less when she was gone, came back sooner, cut his outside life short. I think he could feel I needed him more, needed someone to help me bear the silence of the apartment, the loneliness that overtook me, the tears.

I had to remind myself where I was. College. Working toward a degree in business. Classes were a blur, kind professors extending due dates, the dean stopping by to offer condolences in her calm, impersonal way. My boss at the restaurant where I waited tables was less understanding, letting me know I could take some time but needed to come back soon. No money came in; the small life insurance check only covered the cremation expenses. The cat food supply began to dwindle, and slowly the fridge began to empty, the cabinets holding noodles and not much else.

Then the birds began to arrive.

———

I don't know where he found the variety. Cardinal. Wren. Oriole. Robin. Finch. Others I couldn't identify. I could have looked them up, run my finger down glossy bird books, but I couldn't face that. I didn't want to know if they were rare. If he had made them rarer.

I tried to keep him in at night, making sure the deadbolt was in place. Then I tried a chair and moved a small table to block the only way in and out.

Nothing worked.

———

A blue jay—blue and white, crested, feet curled up, grasping an invisible branch. He lay on the cement in front of the door. I watched it, waiting for the feet to uncurl, an eye to blink. Any sign of life. An ant arrived, sensing death and dinner, forging a path for others to follow.

I moved it to a bush on the side of the building, tucking it beneath the branches, out of the sun. Maybe it would have liked it there. Maybe that's where it had come from. The ant crawled on top of my hand, and I gently blew it off, hoping it would find what it was looking for again.

———

"Onyx, I'm home!"

But he was already there, the jingle of my keys in the

door alerting him, the freedom of the world beyond this tiny space calling. He was through my legs and trotting away before I could stop him. Off to do cat things and live his best cat life.

"Nice to see you too," I said as he disappeared around the corner.

I'd let him in later when he came back to scratch at the door sometime in the middle of the night. Or he'd come to the bedroom window and meow until I got up, strolling inside as if he'd never been gone.

I shut the door and set my bag down, blowing out a sigh, brain mush from a full day of classes and back sore from being on my feet at the restaurant for another five hours afterward. My stomach ached with emptiness, but I was tired enough to choose sleep over food. Exhausted, burning the candle at both ends, praying that I wouldn't fizzle out. I wasn't sure I'd be able to light myself again.

Stumbling to the bedroom, I took off my jeans, shimmying out of them and tossing them with my foot to a pile by the bed. I smelled like fried foods—cheese, pickles, chicken, and ranch dressing. It permeated my skin, my hair, getting under my nails. But I didn't care right now. I took everything else off and crawled into bed, pulling the quilt up and falling asleep almost instantly.

I woke to a rough tongue swiping over my face, smelly cat kisses, the ever-present purr. Onyx, heavy paws on my shoulder, leaning into me, determined to wake me up. I opened one eye, squinting at him, his face close to mine, green eyes, black whiskers tickling.

I glanced at the bedside clock. Just after five in the morning. My alarm would be going off soon anyway. My first class at seven, the ones that came after, a few hours at the library to work on my paper, and work at the restaurant following all of that, jaw already aching from the demanded friendly smile.

Onyx meowed, the sound pitiful and hungry.

But when had I let him inside? I didn't remember getting up, even shuffling to the door half-asleep to let him back in. There had been no meow beyond the window. Nothing.

He jumped off the bed, hurrying away, meowing as he went.

"All right," I said. "I'm getting up. I'll open you a can."

Small cans with pop lids that peeled back, the juices inside sometimes flicking out. I didn't want to know what cat food was made of. Fish. Chicken. Beef. Deep down, I didn't believe it. I'd heard about the pet food documentaries but never watched them. I might try to train my cat to be a vegetarian otherwise.

I was half-asleep still—a lingering dream, the memory of pressure on my chest, then the sudden pull back to consciousness as a rough tongue touched my cheek. The can was light, a nothing weight in my hand, as I turned to get a plate from the cabinet. It dropped whole and unopened, hitting the tile floor, clattering and rolling away.

A sparrow, small and brown, a pattern of delicate shades—a curl of winter leaf or rough rolled bark. It lay on the plate, waiting on the counter, a knife and fork beside it. Limp. Lifeless. Dead. My skin prickled, cold, and then heat touched me, rolling through me as my stomach clenched.

The knife and fork caught the reflection of the overhead kitchen light. The plate was my mother's, something I'd taken from the house of my childhood and carried into my adulthood. It was wrong to have it tinged with death like this, to carry such a delicate meal.

I looked down at him, meeting a steady green gaze.

My mother had said a cat would try to feed you. It sees you as another cat, a stupid cat unable to feed yourself, and will bring you meals until you're able to hunt on your own. Onyx jumped onto the counter and began to purr.

"I don't eat birds," I said, my voice small, coming from a distant place.

The purr stopped. He watched me.

"You know you're not allowed on the counter." I picked him up, heavy and warm, all solid muscle in my arms. I set him on the floor, smoothing his ears down, his eyes closing for a moment.

Leave it. Face it later. Conquer your day first, do the things that must be done. I bent and picked up the can, tapping it onto a plate, gelatinous and uniform. I left the sparrow on the counter, unable to touch it, something in me revolting, closing off.

Onyx rubbed against my leg, the smell of cat food strong in the room, fishy and foul.

He followed me around the apartment, in and out of the bathroom and the closet, looking for my favorite T-shirt. A shadow. A companion. When I left the apartment, pulling the door closed, holding the key and ready to lock it, I caught a glimpse of him jumping onto the sofa and settling down for a bath.

When I came home from work, the dead thing in my apartment was gone. The dish sat in the drying rack, the knife and fork put up.

SHADOW
PART SIX

Awake.

Thick darkness laid over me, heavy like a blanket weighted down for reassurance. This was the opposite of that. Crushing. Something about it familiar, recalling times when I'd woken to find Onyx on my chest, purring into the night, pinning me to the bed.

Something else kept me in place now.

My heart raced, chest tight, instant fight or flight. Pure panic. But where? Where could I go? Why did I need to go? I fought to penetrate the darkness, searching blindly, listening. Pitch-black, no light, no noise. But I could feel it. I was being watched.

Slowly my eyes adjusted, shapes coming forward, as if appearing through mist, fuzzy and indistinct. The bedroom door was open. Had it been closed? I usually kept it closed, needing the security, the moment it would give me if a stranger entered my house.

I moved my legs, searching for Onyx, the warmth of him at the foot of my bed, a comforting presence.

Nothing.

He'd been there as I'd given in to sleep, silently asking the universe to gift it dreamlessly, to hold the confused prophecies that would never come true, the strangeness of stop-motion time. No memories tonight. No last words or jumbled sentences. I had pleaded for it, and it had been answered. But coming back from that place left me slow, head thick, full of sleep.

"Onyx?" I whispered.

Something moved in the hall, feet on carpet, shuffling, coming toward me. Not a small thing. A hulking shape filled the doorframe, darkness within darkness. Huge. Coming when I called, answering me. Faintly glowing green eyes fixed on me, farther up than possible, near the ceiling, reflective like animal eyes.

I sat up, a scream lodged in my throat, a choking sound, and fumbled with my bedside lamp. I could hear it, *please, please, please*. Soft, desperate. The light snapped on, bright light blinding me, relief and fear coming at the same time. Now I would see it, now I would know.

The pleading came from me, soft and raspy, but I didn't recognize my voice. I bit the tip of my tongue, stopping the words, focusing on the pressure. The creature would be there when I turned, when I looked back to the doorway, filling the opening, waiting to step fully into the light. Forcing myself, everything inside me screaming, I turned to the door.

A small black cat. Green eyes. Tail wrapped around his paws, perfectly still.

Onyx.

We sat staring at each other.

All my life, he kept coming out of the dark, through locked doors, from back gardens and dim halls. I looked beyond him to the hall and the long shadows. The outline of a hulking shape, a sharp snout and curved horns, thick quills along a curved back, and a tail. It moved, shifting on its feet, hands limp at its side, with thin clawed fingers.

It was all so clear, as if the shadow being cast was the thing itself.

Onyx yawned, eyes squinting, a flash of sharp white teeth, a pinkish-red tongue.

My cat. The friend of my childhood. My companion.

"Come here," I said, patting the mattress.

An invitation, welcoming, accepting the monster in my house.

He came, a small sound coming from him, pleasure at being invited in and wanted.

When he jumped on the bed, it dipped as if he weighed more, the small body dense with muscle, bones of iron or steel. I reached forward, running my hand over his head, smoothing down his ears. He closed his eyes, content, enjoying the attention, and came toward me, leaning into the contact.

The light remained on as I eased back, pulling the quilt up as he settled beside my hip, purring contentedly. I kept running my hand over his head, down his back, his fur so soft and glossy.

I slept with the light on after that. A grown woman afraid of the dark.

KEYS
PART SEVEN

"Hold the elevator!"

A hand shot between the closing doors, an arm following, then a man pushing inside the small space. My finger hovered over the button that closed the doors, not quick enough to beat him to it. I didn't look at him. No eye contact as I hit the button for the fourth floor of the parking garage where my car waited.

"What floor?" I asked.

"Fourth."

I nodded, adjusting my purse on my shoulder, running an inventory of the contents. Keys. Wallet. Cell phone. Sunglasses. Gum. There was pepper spray in my car, slipped beneath the seat. I kept meaning to fish it out, but I hadn't. Too late.

The man moved to stand behind me. I could just see him out of the corner of my eye. Tall. Dark hair. Jeans and a T-shirt. He was on his phone, scrolling, seeming to ignore me. But my skin crawled.

The elevator rose, rumbling, shimmying up the shaft. I'd had the last appointment of the day. The monthly visit with my psychiatrist. Yes, the medication was working. Yes, my nightmares and anxiety were under control. I'd had to park on the top level, the ceiling low, cars squeezed into tiny slots. But it would be emptier now. Empty.

With a ding, the elevator stopped, the red number four above the door as it slid open. I hesitated, waiting for the stranger to walk past me, to prove me wrong, to go on about his life.

"Go ahead," he said.

I smiled tightly, eyes down, death grip on my purse as I stepped from metal floor to cement. Walk calmly. Casual. You're not in any danger. My keys jingled as I pulled them out, the sound echoing, filled with promise. I couldn't see my car from here, but I knew it was there. Small red car, just around the corner. A few cars still waiting for their owners. Black sedans. Minivans. Huge trucks with thick tires.

Footsteps followed me. Right there, so close. I glanced back, over a shoulder, making a fist around my keys. The man looked down at his phone, scrolling still, reading something as he walked. Texts. News. Memes. He wanted nothing from me. But I looked too long, and he felt my eyes, his gaze flicking up, dark eyes meeting mine.

Nothing there. Nothing human. Nothing. Nothing. Nothing.

Cold swept through me, stomach dropping. Fear, my familiar, my friend, returned. I've missed you. I began to walk faster, looking forward now, hearing him speed up, our footsteps matching, marching in time, filling my ears. A huge truck was blocking the view of my car, but I knew it was there—a bubble of safety.

This couldn't happen. I pressed the key fob, the car beeping, lights flashing. I could feel the lock sliding home already. I knew the pressure of the driver's seat beneath me, the seat belt clicking. A scream crawled up my throat, but my mouth was dry, my chest too tight to pull enough air in to let it escape.

The footsteps behind me grew louder, covering more distance, sneakers on concrete, swift and sure. I did scream finally. Pushing it out, the strangled sound nothing like the wail I'd hoped for, a loud piercing call that might bring someone to me, that might save me. A dry yelp. Weak. But my car was just there, on the other side of the huge truck. I could see the rear end, the shelter it promised.

My shoe hit something, a crack in the pavement, a tiny stone, a nothing. I pitched forward, landing hard on my knees, my hands out to catch me—stinging, the bite of bruised and broken flesh. The man was almost there, almost on me, the sound of him closing in felt in my bones. This is it. I tensed, solid stone, waiting. I squeezed my eyes shut, panting, ready for his hands to land on me, for his breath to hit my neck, for the world to go dark. I would fight. I would get up and run any second. But my muscles were locked.

Please no.

A noise like a meat tenderizer hitting a cheap cut of beef. My mother came to mind, the image of her standing in the kitchen and making chicken fried steaks, a small silver hammer with a spiked surface smacking into red flesh. Again. Over and over. Potatoes bubbling on the stove, hissing and steaming as the water boiled. She turned to me, the small me, the child inside the adult, and smiled.

It hadn't happened.

I opened my eyes, unclenching my jaw, loosening my body to turn and look behind me. Empty. The parking garage was empty. On shaky legs, I stood and turned in a circle, searching the area. I couldn't see him. But there was nowhere for him to go.

My keys were a few feet away, near the truck, close to my car. They'd gone flying when I fell, sliding across the cement. I crossed to them and bent, stopping when something under the truck caught my eye.

A pair of legs was disappearing into the shadows, sliding toward the front of the vehicle, beneath the engine where it was darkest. Jeans. Sneakers. Something wet caught the light, an oil slick, condensation from the air conditioner. Not anything else. Not blood.

My keys jingle-jangled in my hand, stomach turning, feet carrying me to my car without realizing it. The lock I'd so desperately wanted, snapping into place. I was out of the spot with a squeal of tires, driving without watching where I was going, eyes on the white truck in the rearview mirror.

END
PART EIGHT

Greg. Such a normal name. Generic. Greg with his sandy-colored hair and blue eyes, tall enough that I had to look up and stand on tiptoes to kiss him. He never came to me, never reached for me. I was always grasping, always tugging him away from whatever was more important. Everything was more important.

I don't know how I got to the place where he raised his hand. A tense conversation on my sofa, the television volume low, drowned out by raised voices. A muscle in his jaw jumping as I spoke, clenching and unclenching, as more questions came. I wanted commitment, I wanted some-thing more solid than the nights he came to my apartment and left me early in the morning. I wanted something solid beneath my feet, and I'd finally reached a point where I was ready to ask for it.

Afterward, I told myself I'd known better. When the apartment was dark, ice pressed to my lip, already wondering how I would cover up the swollen eye on Monday morning. After he'd gone, I sat on the kitchen floor, shaking, refusing to cry, wincing, and talking to myself.

"You shouldn't have said anything."

"He said he was sorry."

"This is your fault."

Later, after I'd looked in the mirror and pressed a fingertip to my lip so hard blood welled up, I cried. Onyx wove between my legs, rubbing against me, head to tail. When I didn't bend down to pet him, he jumped up, landing on the bathroom counter with a thump. He looked at me, waiting for me to pet him, and when I didn't, he put his front paws on my shoulder, leaning into me, sniffing my face.

"It's okay," I said, petting him finally, smoothing back his ears. "I'm fine."

———

A hissing breath, through clenched teeth, sounding tight and drawn out, someone fighting to hold on to it. I could feel it beneath my breastbone, heart constricting, pounding back into life. I swallowed, mouth dry, that same old feeling creeping up, coming to take my hand.

I know you, it said. *Hello friend.*

Setting down the laundry I was folding into neat piles, I stood. The room around me was a mess. Deep cleaning. Scrubbing Greg out of all of it. New sheets. Clothes in plastic bags to give away. I was starting fresh.

The hissing breath came again, traveling through the quiet air, sounding as if it were on the other side of my closed bedroom door. I steeled myself, hand on the knob, letting go a breath of my own before pulling it open.

The hall was dim, a little light from the windows in the living room coming through. For a moment, it reminded me of another hall, one from my childhood. The door to the bathroom was barely open, just a sliver of light, home to the harsh breath, the desperation. At the end of the hall, sitting perfectly still, was Onyx.

"What did you bring me?" I whispered.

Terror unfolded, curling out like an opening flower, the curl of a fern frond—perfect and tightly green. The cat blinked at me, slow, and waited for me to see for myself. A low groan came from the bathroom, but I couldn't look away from the cat.

He seemed to shrug and gave me a *merp*, stretching as he stood. I clenched my hands, not in anger, but fear, keeping myself from trembling, holding myself so tight. *Don't let go.* Crossing to the bathroom, he paused, shot me a look, and pushed the cracked door open, slipping inside.

I followed, called, summoned, knowing this was the time that counted the most. Out of all the things that had happened over the years, seen and unseen, this was the one that would change how I looked at the world. I thought it had come so many times before, I thought I'd been here and passed it. No. It was now.

I curled my toes into the carpet as I went, putting my hand flat against the door to push it open, the room's tile cold as I entered. My face in the mirror startled me—a fading bruise, a scabbed upper lip. My eyes were wide, pupils dilated, ready to take it all in. Expectation. Impending doom. My shoulders hunched beneath a painful weight, the contents of this room something to carry into the future.

A noise. Bubbling. Hissing.

Turning to the tub, I kept my eyes on the tiled floor—white tile, little woven dark blue rugs in front of the sink and the tub. Blue towels to match. The toilet. The shower curtain pulled aside.

Something in the tub.

Onyx jumped up, landing on the edge, walking along it delicately, inspecting. He meowed, and I sagged, knees shaking. He looked from me to the tub and back, back and forth between myself and what lay in the tub.

Red. Deep and rich, vibrant and dark. It reminded me of split lips and open wounds, a dark splash on pavement, a smear on a severed ear. I sucked in a breath, another, fighting to keep my lungs full, sweat prickling in my armpits.

Cats will bring you half-dead things to teach you to hunt. They see you as another cat. Except you're an idiot who hasn't figured out how to hunt for yourself. They bring mice covered in puncture wounds, small rabbits with cracked necks, birds with broken wings—still breathing, living, desperate to escape the predator, waiting for a chance that will never come.

The thing in the tub was alive too.

Thing. Did it have a name anymore? Greg.

Breath bubbled out, his mouth torn open, split, the pink flesh of the cheeks exposed. Mad eyes, not angry, but full of fear, whites showing, rolling toward the cat, the bubbling breath turning into a choking, retching sound. Puncture wounds on his shoulder and chest, his lower body twisted at an unnatural angle. One arm barely attached, the fingers on the other hand opening and closing on nothing.

No more fists, no more backhanded slaps.

No more, no more, no more.

It circled through me, and all I felt was relief.

Onyx jumped down, coming toward me, looking up to see what I thought. *Are you pleased?* Behind him, Greg's mouth was moving, a bloody hole, missing teeth, fighting to come together, to form words, to scream, to make any other sound than that hissing, bubbling tortured breathing.

I couldn't go any closer. I couldn't turn back. Call for help. Call for help. My cell phone was in my bedroom, forgotten along with the pile of clothes. Beyond these walls were other people, someone who would help Greg.

But.

What would I tell them? How would I explain my face? The bloody ex-boyfriend in my tub? There would be questions, faces pinched tight around suspicion, minds made up, decisions made. I would get one phone call. But I had no one to call.

The air in the room shifted, moving as something expanded, taking up space. The thing in the tub made a sound it hadn't before. Almost a yelp, louder than anything else so far. If it could have moved, it would have, even now, it seemed to vibrate against the porcelain, and I had to look away.

A large hand came to rest on my shoulder, gentle, the soft prick of claws resting against my flesh. There was height and muscle at my back, warmth and something like security, like safety. He breathed out, ruffling my hair, the scent of copper coming with it, fresh blood.

A muscled forearm came into view, covered in fine black fur, knobby fingers tipped with long black claws so sharp they cut the air as he pointed toward the tub. I turned slightly to see a shoulder covered in the same fur, the bulk of a dark body, a sharp face. *He.* But he turned me back away from him—away from the monster that lived under my bed, the cat that followed me to the kitchen each morning for a can of smelly cat food. He urged me toward the tub, his chest to my back, as I took a stumbling step.

Look what I brought you.

I began to tremble, bile rising in my throat. I shook my head, a noise I didn't recognize coming from me. The thing in the tub gurgled, focused on the huge dark figure behind me, touching me. I was urged forward again, shown my meal, expected to eat. To finish what had been started.

"No," I said softly, shaking my head.

He made a noise, a question, so like the *merp* in the hall.

"I can't."

Let me.

I nodded. Yes. Yes, I would let him take care of it. I closed my eyes, squeezing them so tight, my face scrunched, keeping it all out. He turned me toward the door, guided me through it, pushed me into the dim hall, and sent me stumbling toward my room.

Behind me. Behind me were noises.

The air conditioner came on, cool air touching me, ruffling my hair as I passed beneath a vent in the hall. Evening light came to me from the bedroom, the curtains pulled back, gold and pink waiting to engulf me. Take me in. Give me something warm after the fluorescent glare of the bathroom; bare tile, wide eyes, deep red arterial blood. Heart's blood.

I lay down on my bed, on top of the quilt in various shades of green, rolling onto my side to face the window and watch the setting sun—knees up, arms curled in. The sounds from the bathroom continued, going on until I thought they'd never stop, thinking I would live the rest of my life with those noises in my head. Wet chewing. The snap of a bone, cracking, marrow slurped. Then quieting, fading.

The bathroom door opened, and I closed my eyes, squeezing them tight, refusing even to see the black world on the other side of my eyelids. I kept them closed as the air in the room changed, holding my breath as the bed dipped behind me, taking on weight. He fit himself to me, chest to back, knees tucked up with mine, arm coming over to take my hand, engulfing me.

Onyx began to purr.

ABOUT THE AUTHOR

Kathryn Trattner has loved fairy tales, folk stories, and mythology all of her life. Her hands down favorites have always been East of the Sun, West of the Moon, and the story of Persephone and Hades. When not writing or reading she's traveling as much as possible and taking thousands of photos that probably won't get edited later. She lives in Oklahoma with her wonderful partner, two very busy children, one of the friendliest dogs ever, and an extremely grumpy cat who doesn't like anyone at all.

Thank you for reading!

Want all the latest new release info? Join my newsletter!
https://www.kathryntrattner.com/newsletter

 facebook.com/kathryntrattner

twitter.com/k_trattner

instagram.com/k.trattner.author

bookbub.com/authors/kathryn-trattner

pinterest.com/kathryntrattner

ALSO BY KATHRYN TRATTNER

Deep Water and Other Stories

Mistress of Death

The Scent of Leaves

The Glass Palace

Magnolia House

<u>Blood and Rubies Series</u>

The Dead Saint

The Living Saint

Steel and Starlight

www.ingramcontent.com/pod-product-compliance
Lightning Source LLC
Chambersburg PA
CBHW022042170626
46808CB00003B/1337